To all children . . . trust your feelings
JAK

For Oscar
CD

Thank you to the Bank Street Writers Lab
for their support and encouragement. –JAK

First edition 2020

Library of Congress Catalog Card Number pending
ISBN 978-0-7636-9832-4

CCP 25 24 23 22 21 20
10 9 8 7 6 5 4 3 2 1

Printed in Shenzhen, Guangdong, China

This book was typeset in Berkeley.
The illustrations were created in watercolor, gouache,
India ink, and digital collage.

Candlewick Press
99 Dover Street
Somerville, Massachusetts 02144

www.candlewick.com

# The Boy and the Gorilla

Jackie Azúa Kramer

*illustrated by* Cindy Derby

CANDLEWICK PRESS

Your mother's garden is beautiful.
May I help?

Okay.

My mom died.

*I know.*

How do you know when someone dies?

*A person's body stops working.*

Like their heartbeat?

*Yes.*

Will we all die?

*Yes. We all do. But you have many more kites to fly.*

Where did Mom go?

*No one knows for sure.*

Maybe Mom's here. She liked the waves.

Can't my mom come back home?

*No. But she's always with you.*

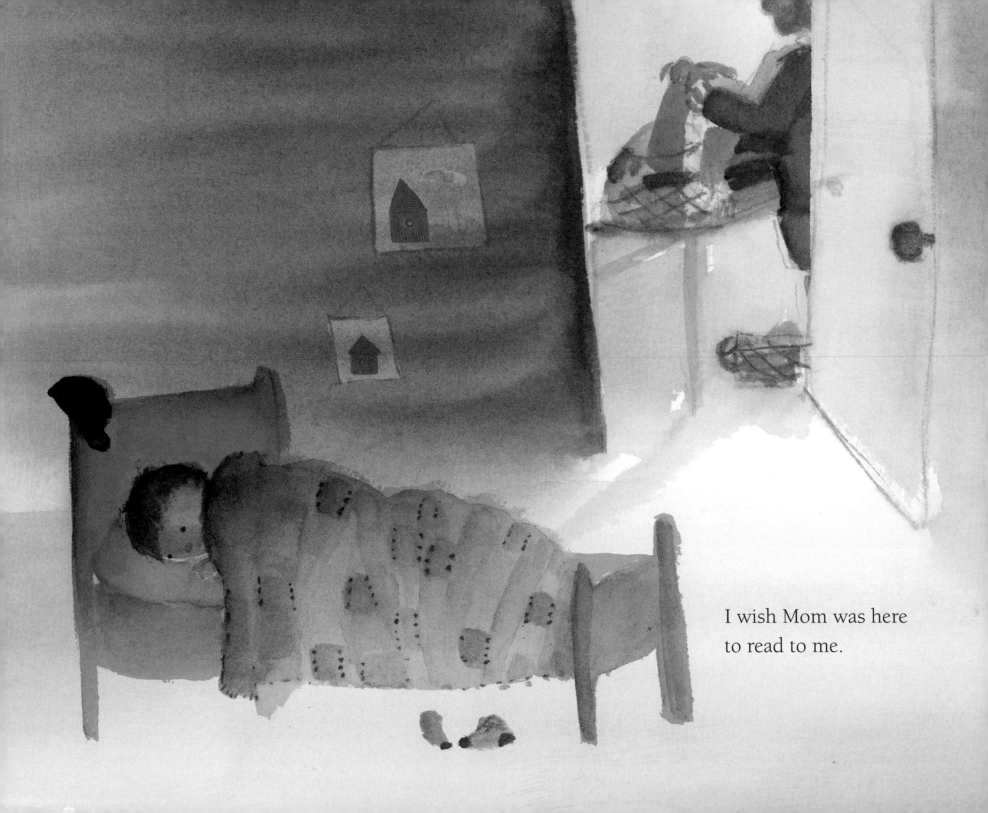

I wish Mom was here
to read to me.

It's a good story.
Your father might like this book, too.

I like Mom's pancakes better.

Sometimes I want to be alone.

*That's all right. Everyone needs quiet time.*

I'm going to climb to the top!
Maybe Mom will be there!

*I'm right behind you.*

Why did she have to die?

*All living things die. It hurts not to be able to be with someone we love.*

When will I feel better?

*When you know she's still with you.*

Mom and I loved baseball.

*That's it. She's with you when you play.*

You mean like baking Mom's special cookies?

*Yes, each bite is like a memory.*

Or picking daisies from Mom's garden?

*The seeds you planted together are like your mother's love, a gift to keep forever.*

Dad . . .

I miss Mom.

Mom had a funny laugh.

*And she told the best jokes.*
*I miss your mother, too.*

*But I can see her in your smile.*

Mom will like her new flowers.